BLACK COLOSSUS

BY

ROBERT E. HOWARD

British Library Cataloguing-in-Publication Data
A catalogue record for this book is available from the
British Library

Contents

Robert E. Howard

Robert Ervin Howard was born in Peaster, Texas in 1906. During his youth, his family moved between a variety of Texan boomtowns, and Howard – a bookish and somewhat introverted child – was steeped in the violent myths and legends of the Old South. Although he loved reading and learning, Howard developed a distinctly Texan, hardboiled outlook on the world. He became a passionate fan of boxing, taking it up at an amateur level, and from the age of nine began to write adventure tales of semi-historical bloodshed. In 1919, when Howard was thirteen, his family moved to the Central Texas hamlet of Cross Plains, where he would stay for the rest of his life.

At fifteen Howard began to read the pulp magazines of the day, and to write more seriously. The December 1922 issue of his high school newspaper featured two of his stories, 'Golden Hope Christmas' and 'West is West'. In 1924 he sold his first piece – a short caveman tale titled 'Spear and Fang' – for $16 to the not-yet-famous *Weird Tales* magazine. He published with the magazine regularly over the next few years. 1929 was a breakout year for Howard, in that the 23-year-old writer began to sell to other magazines, such as *Ghost Stories* and *Argosy*, both of whom had previously sent him hundreds of rejection slips. In 1930, he began a correspondence with weird fiction master H. P. Lovecraft which ran up to his death six years later, and is regarded as one of the great correspondence cycles in all of fantasy literature.

It was partly due to Lovecraft's encouragement that Howard created his most famous character, Conan the Cimmerian. Conan – a barbarian-turned-King during the Hyborian Age, a mythical period of some 12,000 years ago – featured in seventeen *Weird Tales* stories between 1933 and 1936, and is now regarded as having spawned the 'sword and sorcery' genre, making Howard's influence on fantasy literature comparable to that of J. R. R. Tolkien's. The Conan stories have since been adapted many times, most famously in the series of films starring Arnold Schwarzenegger.

Howard was enjoying an all-time high in sales by the beginning of 1936, but he was also deeply upset by the ill health of his mother, who had fallen into a coma. On the morning of June 11, 1936, he asked an attending nurse whether she would ever recover, and the nurse replied negatively. Howard walked to his car, parked outside the family home in Cross Plains, and shot himself. He died eight hours later, aged just thirty.

CHAPTER I

"The Night of Power, when Fate stalked through the corridors of the world like a colossus just risen from an age-old throne of granite—"

E. Hoffman Price: The Girl from Samarcand

Only the age-old silence brooded over the mysterious ruins of Kuthchemes, but Fear was there; Fear quivered in the mind of Shevatas, the thief, driving his breath quick and sharp against his clenched teeth.

He stood, the one atom of life amidst the colossal monuments of desolation and decay. Not even a vulture hung like a black dot in the vast blue vault of the sky that the sun glazed with its heat. On every hand rose the grim relics of another, forgotten age: huge broken pillars, thrusting up their jagged pinnacles into the sky; long wavering lines of crumbling walls; fallen cyclopean blocks of stone; shattered images, whose horrific features the corroding winds and dust-storms had half erased. From horizon to horizon no sign of life: only the sheer breathtaking sweep of the naked desert, bisected by the wandering line of a long-dry river course; in the midst of that vastness the glimmering fangs of the ruins, the columns standing up like broken masts of sunken ships—all dominated by the towering ivory dome before which Shevatas stood trembling.

The base of this dome was a gigantic pedestal of marble rising from what had once been a terraced eminence on the banks of the ancient river. Broad steps led up to a great bronze door in the dome, which rested on its base like the half of some titanic egg. The dome itself was of pure ivory, which shone as if unknown hands kept it polished. Likewise shone the spired gold cap of the pinnacle, and the inscription which sprawled about the curve of the dome in golden hieroglyphics yards long. No man on earth could read those characters, but Shevatas shuddered at the dim conjectures they raised. For he came of a very old race, whose myths ran back to shapes undreamed of by contemporary tribes.

Shevatas was wiry and lithe, as became a master-thief of Zamora. His small round head was shaven, his only garment a loin-cloth of scarlet silk. Like all his race, he was very dark, his narrow vulture-like face set off by his keen black eyes. His long, slender and tapering fingers were quick and nervous as the wings of a moth. From a gold-scaled girdle hung a short, narrow, jewel-hilted sword in a sheath of ornamented leather. Shevatas handled the weapon with apparently exaggerated care. He even seemed to flinch away from the contact of the sheath with his naked thigh. Nor was his care without reason.

This was Shevatas, a thief among thieves, whose name was spoken with awe in the dives of the Maul and the dim shadowy recesses beneath the temples of Bel, and who lived in songs and myths for a thousand years. Yet fear ate at the heart of Shevatas as he stood before the ivory dome of Kuthchemes. Any fool could see there was something unnatural about the structure; the winds and suns of three thousand years had lashed it, yet its gold and ivory rose bright and glistening as the day it was reared by nameless hands on the bank of the nameless river.

This unnaturalness was in keeping with the general aura of these devil-haunted ruins. This desert was the mysterious expanse lying southeast of the lands of Shem. A few days' ride on camel-back to the southwest, as Shevatas knew, would bring the traveller within sight of the great river Styx at the point where it turned at right angles with its former course, and flowed westward to empty at last into the distant sea. At the point of its bend began the land of Stygia, the dark-bosomed mistress of the south, whose domains, watered by the great river, rose sheer out of the surrounding desert.

Eastward, Shevatas knew, the desert shaded into steppes stretching to the Hyrkanian kingdom of Turan, rising in barbaric splendor on the shores of the great inland sea. A week's ride northward the desert ran into a tangle of barren hills, beyond which lay the fertile uplands of Koth, the southernmost realm of the Hyborian races. Westward the desert merged into the meadowlands of Shem, which stretched away to the ocean.

All this Shevatas knew without being particularly conscious of the knowledge, as a man knows the streets of his town. He was a far traveller and had looted the treasures of many kingdoms. But now he hesitated and shuddered before the highest adventure and the mightiest treasure of all.

In that ivory dome lay the bones of Thugra Khotan, the dark sorcerer who had reigned in Kuthchemes three thousand years ago, when the kingdoms of Stygia stretched far northward of the great river, over the meadows of Shem, and into the uplands. Then the great drift of the Hyborians swept southward from the cradle-land of their race near the northern pole. It was a titanic drift, extending over centuries and ages. But in the reign of Thugra Khotan, the last magician of Kuthchemes, gray-eyed, tawny-haired barbarians in wolfskins and scale-mail had ridden from the north into the rich uplands to carve out the kingdom of Koth with their iron swords. They had stormed over Kuthchemes like a tidal wave, washing the marble towers in blood, and the northern Stygian kingdom had gone down in fire and ruin.

But while they were shattering the streets of his city and cutting down his archers like ripe corn, Thugra Khotan had swallowed a strange terrible poison, and his masked priests had locked him into the tomb he himself had prepared.

His devotees died about that tomb in a crimson holocaust, but the barbarians could not burst the door, nor ever mar the structure by maul or fire. So they rode away, leaving the great city in ruins, and in his ivory-domed sepulcher great Thugra Khotan slept unmolested, while the lizards of desolation gnawed at the crumbling pillars, and the very river that watered his land in old times sank into the sands and ran dry.

Many a thief sought to gain the treasure which fables said lay heaped about the moldering bones inside the dome. And many a thief died at the door of the tomb, and many another was harried by monstrous dreams to die at last with the froth of madness on his lips.

So Shevatas shuddered as he faced the tomb, nor was his shudder altogether occasioned by the legend of the serpent said to guard the sorcerer's bones. Over all myths of Thugra Khotan hung horror and death like a pall. From where the thief stood he could see the ruins of the great hall wherein chained captives had knelt by the hundreds during festivals to have their heads hacked off by the priest-king in honor of Set, the Serpent-god of Stygia. Somewhere near by had been the pit, dark and awful, wherein screaming victims were fed to a nameless amorphic monstrosity which came up out of a deeper, more hellish cavern. Legend made Thugra Khotan more than human; his worship yet lingered in a mongrel degraded cult, whose votaries stamped his likeness on coins to pay the way of their dead over the great river of darkness of which the Styx was but the material shadow. Shevatas had seen this likeness, on coins stolen from under the tongues of the dead, and its image was etched indelibly in his brain.

But he put aside his fears and mounted to the bronze door, whose smooth surface offered no bolt or catch. Not for naught had he gained access into darksome cults, had harkened to the grisly whispers of the votaries of Skelos under midnight trees, and read the forbidden iron-bound books of Vathelos the Blind.

Kneeling before the portal, he searched the sill with nimble fingers; their sensitive tips found projections too small for the eye to detect, or for less-skilled fingers to discover. These he pressed carefully and according to a peculiar system, muttering a long-forgotten incantation as he did so. As he pressed the last projection, he sprang up with frantic haste and struck the exact center of the door a quick sharp blow with his open hand.

There was no rasp of spring or hinge, but the door retreated inward, and the breath hissed explosively from Shevatas's clenched teeth. A short narrow corridor was disclosed. Down this the door had slid, and was now in place at the other end. The floor, ceiling and sides of the tunnel-like aperture were of ivory, and now from an opening on one side came a silent writhing horror that reared up and glared on the intruder with awful luminous eyes; a serpent twenty feet long, with shimmering, iridescent scales.

The thief did not waste time in conjecturing what night-black pits lying below the dome had given sustenance to the monster. Gingerly he drew the sword, and from it dripped a greenish liquid exactly like that which slavered from the scimitar-fangs of the reptile. The blade was steeped in the poison of the snake's own kind, and the obtaining of that venom from the fiend-haunted swamps of Zingara would have made a saga in itself.

Shevatas advanced warily on the balls of his feet, knees bent slightly, ready to spring either way like a flash of light. And he needed all his co-ordinate speed when the snake arched its neck and struck, shooting out its full length like a stroke of lightning. For all his quickness of nerve and eye, Shevatas had died then but for chance. His well-laid plans of leaping aside and striking down on the outstretched neck were put at naught by the blinding speed of the reptile's attack. The thief had but time to extend the sword in front of him, involuntarily closing his eyes and crying out. Then the sword was wrenched from his hand and the corridor was filled with a horrible thrashing and lashing.

Opening his eyes, amazed to find himself still alive, Shevatas saw the monster heaving and twisting its slimy form in fantastic contortions, the sword transfixing its giant jaws. Sheer chance had hurled it full against the point he had held out blindly. A few moments later the serpent sank into shining, scarcely quivering coils, as the poison on the blade struck home.

Gingerly stepping over it, the thief thrust against the door, which this time slid aside, revealing the interior of the dome. Shevatas cried out; instead of utter darkness he had come into a crimson light that throbbed and pulsed almost beyond the endurance of mortal eyes. It came from a gigantic red jewel high up in the vaulted arch of the dome. Shevatas gaped, inured though he was to the sight of riches. The treasure was there, heaped in staggering profusion—piles of diamonds, sapphires, rubies, turquoises, opals, emeralds; ziggurats of jade, jet and lapis lazuli; pyramids of gold wedges; teocallis of silver ingots; jewel-hilted swords in cloth-of-gold sheaths; golden helmets with colored horsehair crests, or black and scarlet plumes; silver scaled corselets; gem-crusted harness worn by warrior-kings three thousand years in their tombs; goblets carven of single jewels; skulls plated with gold, with moonstones for eyes; necklaces of human teeth set with jewels. The ivory floor was covered inches deep with gold dust that sparkled and shimmered under the crimson glow with a million scintillant lights. The thief stood in a wonderland of magic and splendor, treading stars under his sandalled feet.

But his eyes were focussed on the dais of crystal which rose in the midst of the shimmering array, directly under the red jewel, and on which should be lying the moldering bones, turning to dust with the crawling of the centuries. And as Shevatas looked, the blood drained from his dark features; his marrow turned to ice, and the skin of his back crawled and wrinkled with horror, while his lips worked soundlessly. But suddenly he found his voice in one awful scream that rang hideously under the arching dome. Then again the silence of the ages lay among the ruins of mysterious Kuthchemes.

CHAPTER II

Rumors drifted up through the meadowlands, into the cities of the Hyborians. The word ran along the caravans, the long camel-trains plodding through the sands, herded by lean, hawkeyed men in white kaftans. It was passed on by the hook-nosed herdsmen of the grasslands, from the dwellers in tents to the dwellers in the squat stone cities where kings with curled blueblack beards worshipped round-bellied gods with curious rites. The word passed up through the fringe of hills where gaunt tribesmen took toll of the caravans. The rumors came into the fertile uplands where stately cities rose above blue lakes and rivers: the rumors marched along the broad white roads thronged with ox-wains, with lowing herds, with rich merchants, knights in steel, archers and priests.

They were rumors from the desert that lies east of Stygia, far south of the Kothian hills. A new prophet had risen among the nomads. Men spoke of tribal war, of a gathering of vultures in the southeast, and a terrible leader who led his swiftly increasing hordes to victory. The Stygians, ever a menace to the northern nations, were apparently not connected with this movement; for they were massing armies on their eastern borders and their priests were making magic to fight that of the desert sorcerer, whom men called Natohk, the Veiled One; for his features were always masked.

But the tide swept northwestward, and the blue-bearded kings died before the altars of their pot-bellied gods, and their squat-walled cities were drenched in blood. Men said that the uplands of the Hyborians were the goal of Natohk and his chanting votaries.

Raids from the desert were not uncommon, but this latest movement seemed to promise more than a raid. Rumor said Natohk had welded thirty nomadic tribes and fifteen cities into his following, and that a rebellious Stygian prince had joined him. This latter lent the affair an aspect of real war.

Characteristically, most of the Hyborian nations were prone to ignore the growing menace. But in Khoraja, carved out of Shemite lands by the swords of Kothic adventurers, heed was given. Lying southeast of Koth, it would bear the brunt of the invasion. And its young king was captive to the treacherous king of Ophir, who hesitated between restoring him for a huge ransom, or handing him over to his enemy, the penurious king of Koth, who offered no gold, but an advantageous treaty. Meanwhile, the rule of the struggling kingdom was in the white hands of young princess Yasmela, the king's sister.

Minstrels sang her beauty throughout the western world, and the pride of a kingly dynasty was hers. But on that night her pride was dropped from her like a cloak. In her chamber whose ceiling was a lapis lazuli dome, whose marble floor was littered with rare furs, and whose walls were lavish with golden friezework, ten girls, daughters of nobles, their slender limbs weighted with gem-crusted armlets and anklets, slumbered on velvet couches about the royal bed with its golden dais and silken canopy. But princess Yasmela lolled not on that silken bed. She lay naked on her supple belly upon the bare marble like the most abased suppliant, her dark hair streaming over her white shoulders, her slender fingers intertwined. She lay and writhed in pure horror that froze the blood in her lithe limbs and dilated her beautiful eyes, that pricked the roots of her dark hair and made goose-flesh rise along her supple spine.

Above her, in the darkest corner of the marble chamber, lurked a vast shapeless shadow. It was no living thing of form or flesh and blood. It was a clot of darkness, a blur in the sight, a monstrous night-born incubus that might have been deemed a figment of a sleep-drugged brain, but for the points of blazing yellow fire that glimmered like two eyes from the blackness.

Moreover, a voice issued from it—a low subtle inhuman sibilance that was more like the soft abominable hissing of a serpent than anything else, and that apparently could not emanate from anything with human lips. Its sound as well as its import filled Yasmela with a shuddering horror so intolerable that she writhed and twisted her slender body as

14

if beneath a lash, as though to rid her mind of its insinuating vileness by physical contortion.

"You are marked for mine, princess," came the gloating whisper. "Before I wakened from the long sleep I had marked you, and yearned for you, but I was held fast by the ancient spell by which I escaped mine enemies. I am the soul of Natohk, the Veiled One! Look well upon me, princess! Soon you shall behold me in my bodily guise, and shall love me!"

The ghostly hissing dwindled off in lustful titterings, and Yasmela moaned and beat the marble tiles with her small fists in her ecstasy of terror.

"I sleep in the palace chamber of Akbatana," the sibilances continued. "There my body lies in its frame of bones and flesh. But it is but an empty shell from which the spirit has flown for a brief space. Could you gaze from that palace casement you would realize the futility of resistance. The desert is a rose garden beneath the moon, where blossom the fires of a hundred thousand warriors. As an avalanche sweeps onward, gathering bulk and momentum, I will sweep into the lands of mine ancient enemies. Their kings shall furnish me skulls for goblets, their women and children shall be slaves of my slaves' slaves. I have grown strong in the long years of dreaming . . .

"But thou shalt be my queen, oh princess! I will teach thee the ancient forgotten ways of pleasure. We—" Before the stream of cosmic obscenity which poured from the shadowy colossus, Yasmela cringed and writhed as if from a whip that flayed her dainty bare flesh.

"Remember!" whispered the horror. "The days will not be many before I come to claim mine own!"

Yasmela, pressing her face against the tiles and stopping her pink ears with her dainty fingers, yet seemed to hear a strange sweeping noise, like the beat of bat wings. Then, looking fearfully up, she saw only the moon that shone through the window with a beam that rested like a silver sword across the spot where the phantom had lurked. Trembling in every limb, she rose and staggered to a satin couch, where she threw herself down, weeping hysterically. The girls slept on, but one, who roused, yawned, stretched her slender figure and blinked about. Instantly she was on her knees beside the couch, her arms about Yasmela's supple waist.

"Was it—was it—?" Her dark eyes were wide with fright. Yasmela caught her in a convulsive grasp.

"Oh, Vateesa. It came again! I saw It—heard It speak! It spoke Its name—Natohk! It is Natohk! It is not a nightmare—it towered over me while the girls slept like drugged ones. What oh, what shall I do?"

Vateesa twisted a golden bracelet about her rounded arm in meditation.

"Oh, princess," she said, "it is evident that no mortal power can deal with It, and the charm is useless that the

16

priests of Ishtar gave you. Therefore seek you the forgotten oracle of Mitra."

In spite of her recent fright, Yasmela shuddered. The gods of yesterday become the devils of tomorrow. The Kothians had long since abandoned the worship of Mitra, forgetting the attributes of the universal Hyborian god. Yasmela had a vague idea that, being very ancient, it followed that the deity was very terrible. Ishtar was much to be feared, and all the gods of Koth. Kothian culture and religion had suffered from a subtle admix ture of Shemite and Stygian strains. The simple ways of the Hyborians had become modified to a large extent by the sensual, luxurious, yet despotic habits of the East.

"Will Mitra aid me?" Yasmela caught Vateesa's wrist in her eagerness. "We have worshipped Ishtar so long—"

"To be sure he will!" Vateesa was the daughter of an Ophirean priest who had brought his customs with him when he fled from political enemies to Khoraja. "Seek the shrine! I will go with you."

"I will!" Yasmela rose, but objected when Vateesa prepared to dress her. "It is not fitting that I come before the shrine clad in silk. I will go naked, on my knees, as befits a suppliant, lest Mitra deem I lack humility."

"Nonsense!" Vateesa had scant respect for the ways of what she deemed a false cult. "Mitra would have folks stand upright before him—not crawling on their bellies like worms, or spilling blood of animals all over his altars."

Thus objurgated, Yasmela allowed the girl to garb her in the light sleeveless silk shirt, over which was slipped a silken tunic, bound at the waist by a wide velvet girdle. Satin slippers were put upon her slender feet, and a few deft touches of Vateesa's pink fingers arranged her dark wavy tresses. Then the princess followed the girl, who drew aside a heavy gilt-worked tapestry and threw the golden bolt of the door it concealed. This let into a narrow winding corridor, and down this the two girls went swiftly, through another door and into a broad hallway. Here stood a guardsman in crested gilt helmet, silvered cuirass and gold-chased greaves, with a long-shafted battle-ax in his hands.

A motion from Yasmela checked his exclamation and, saluting, he took his stand again beside the doorway, motionless as a brazen image. The girls traversed the hallway, which seemed immense and eery in the light of the cressets along the lofty walls, and went down a stairway where Yasmela shivered at the blots of shadows which hung in the angles of the walls. Three levels down they halted at last in a narrow corridor whose arched ceiling was crusted with jewels, whose floor was set with blocks of crystal, and whose walls were decorated with golden friezework. Down this shining way they stole, holding each other's hands, to a wide portal of gilt.

Vateesa thrust open the door, revealing a shrine long forgotten except by a faithful few, and royal visitors to Khoraja's court, mainly for whose benefit the fane was maintained. Yasmela had never entered it before, though she was born in the palace. Plain and unadorned in comparison to the lavish display of Ishtar's shrines, there was about it a simplicity of dignity and beauty characteristic of the Mitran religion.

The ceiling was lofty, but it was not domed, and was of plain white marble, as were the walls and floor, the former with a narrow gold frieze running about them. Behind an altar of clear green jade, unstained with sacrifice, stood the pedestal whereon sat the material manifestation of the deity. Yasmela looked in awe at the sweep of the magnificent shoulders, the clear-cut features—the wide straight eyes, the patriarchal beard, the thick curls of the hair, confined by a simple band about the temples. This, though she did not know it, was art in its highest form the free, uncramped artistic expression of a highly esthetic race, unhampered by conventional symbolism.

She fell on her knees and thence prostrate, regardless of Vateesa's admonition, and Vateesa, to be on the safe side, followed her example; for after all, she was only a girl, and it was very awesome in Mitra's shrine. But even so she could not refrain from whispering in Yasmela's ear.

"This is but the emblem of the god. None pretends to know what Mitra looks like. This but represents him in idealized human form, as near perfection as the human mind can conceive. He does not inhabit this cold stone, as your priests tell you Ishtar does. He is everywhere—above us, and about us, and he dreams betimes in the high places among the stars. But here his being focusses. Therefore call upon him."

"What shall I say?" whispered Yasmela in stammering terror.

"Before you can speak, Mitra knows the contents of your mind—" began Vateesa. Then both girls started violently as a voice began in the air above them. The deep, calm, bell-like tones emanated no more from the image than from anywhere else in the chamber. Again Yasmela trembled before a bodiless voice speaking to her, but this time it was not from horror or repulsion.

"Speak not, my daughter, for I know your need," came the intonations like deep musical waves beating rhythmically along a golden beach. "In one manner may you save your kingdom, and saving it, save all the world from the fangs of the serpent which has crawled up out of the darkness of the ages. Go forth upon the streets alone, and place your kingdom in the hands of the first man you meet there."

The unechoing tones ceased, and the girls stared at each other. Then, rising, they stole forth, nor did they speak until they stood once more in Yasmela's chamber. The princess stared out of the gold-barred windows. The moon had set. It was long past midnight. Sounds of revelry had died away in the gardens and on the roofs of the city. Khoraja slumbered beneath the stars, which seemed to be reflected in the cressets that twinkled among the gardens and along the streets and on the flat roofs of houses where folk slept.

"What will you do?" whispered Vateesa, all a-tremble.

"Give me my cloak," answered Yasmela, setting her teeth.

"But alone, in the streets, at this hour!" expostulated Vateesa.

"Mitra has spoken," replied the princess. "It might have been the voice of the god, or a trick of a priest. No matter. I will go!"

Wrapping a voluminous silken cloak about her lithe figure and donning a velvet cap from which depended a filmy veil, she passed hurriedly through the corridors and approached a bronze door where a dozen spearmen gaped at her as she passed through. This was in a wing of the palace which let directly onto the street; on all other sides it was surrounded by broad gardens, bordered by a high wall. She emerged into the street, lighted by cressets placed at regular intervals.

She hesitated; then, before her resolution could falter, she closed the door behind her. A slight shudder shook her as she glanced up and down the street, which lay silent and bare. This daughter of aristocrats had never before ventured unattended outside her ancestral palace. Then, steeling herself, she went swiftly up the street. Her satin-slippered feet fell lightly on the pave, but their soft sound brought her heart into her throat. She imagined their fall echoing thunderously through the cavernous city, rousing ragged rat-eyed figures in hidden lairs among the sewers. Every shadow seemed to hide a lurking assassin, every blank doorway to mask the slinking hounds of darkness.

Then she started violently. Ahead of her a figure appeared on the eery street. She drew quickly into a clump of shadows, which now seemed like a haven of refuge, her pulse pounding. The approaching figure went not furtively, like a thief, or timidly, like a fearful traveller. He strode down the nighted street as one who has no need or desire to walk softly. An unconscious swagger was in his stride, and his footfalls resounded on the pave. As he passed near a cresset she saw him plainly—a tall man, in the chain-mail hauberk of a mercenary. She braced herself, then darted from the shadow, holding her cloak close about her.

"Sa-ha!" his sword flashed half out of his sheath. It halted when he saw it was only a woman that stood before him, but his quick glance went over her head, seeking the shadows for possible confederates.

He stood facing her, his hand on the long hilt that jutted forward from beneath the scarlet cloak which flowed carelessly from his mailed shoulders. The torchlight glinted dully on the polished blue steel of his greaves and basinet. A more baleful fire glittered bluely in his eyes. At first glance she saw he was no Kothian; when he spoke she knew he was no Hyborian. He was clad like a captain of the mercenaries, and in that desperate command there were men of many lands, barbarians as well as civilized foreigners. There was a wolfishness about this warrior that marked the barbarian. The eyes of no civilized man, however wild or criminal, ever blazed with such a fire. Wine scented his breath, but he neither staggered nor stammered.

"Have they shut you into the street?" he asked in barbarous Kothic, reaching for her. His fingers closed lightly about her rounded wrist, but she felt that he could splinter its bones without effort. "I've but come from the last wine-shop open. Ishtar's curse on these white-livered reformers who close the grog-houses! 'Let men sleep rather than guzzle,' they say—aye, so they can work and fight better for their masters! Soft-gutted eunuchs, I call them. When I served with the mercenaries of Corinthia we swilled and wenched all night and fought all day—aye, blood ran down the channels of our swords. But what of you, my girl? Take off that cursed mask—"

She avoided his clutch with a lithe twist of her body, trying not to appear to repulse him. She realized her danger, alone with a drunken barbarian. If she revealed her identity, he might laugh at her, or take himself off. She was not sure he would not cut her throat. Barbaric men did strange inexplicable things. She fought a rising fear.

"Not here," she laughed. "Come with me—"

"Where?" His wild blood was up, but he was wary as a wolf. "Are you taking me to some den of robbers?"

"No, no, I swear it!" She was hard put to avoid the hand which was again fumbling at her veil.

"Devil bite you, hussy!" he growled disgustedly. "You're as bad as a Hyrkanian woman, with your damnable veil. Here—let me look at your figure, anyway."

Before she could prevent it, he wrenched the cloak from her, and she heard his breath hiss between his teeth. He stood holding the cloak, eyeing her as if the sight of her rich garments had somewhat sobered him. She saw suspicion flicker sullenly in his eyes.

"Who the devil are you?" he muttered. "You're no street-waif—unless your leman robbed the king's seraglio for your clothes."

"Never mind." She dared to lay her white hand on his massive iron-clad arm. "Come with me off the street."

He hesitated, then shrugged his mighty shoulders. She saw that he half believed her to be some noble lady, who, weary of polite lovers, was taking this means of amusing herself. He allowed her to don the cloak again, and followed her. From the corner of her eye she watched him as they went down the street together. His mail could not conceal his hard lines of tigerish strength. Everything about him was tigerish, elemental, untamed. He was alien as the jungle to her in his difference from the debonair courtiers to whom she was accustomed. She feared him, told herself she loathed his raw brute strength and unashamed barbarism, yet something breathless and perilous inside her leaned toward him; the hidden primitive chord that lurks in every woman's soul was sounded and responded. She had felt his hardened hand on her arm, and something deep in her tingled to the memory of that contact. Many men had knelt before Yasmela. Here was one she felt had never knelt before any one. Her sensations were those of one leading an unchained tiger; she was frightened, and fascinated by her fright.

She halted at the palace door and thrust lightly against it. Furtively watching her companion, she saw no suspicion in his eyes.

"Palace, eh?" he rumbled. "So you're a maid-in-waiting?"

She found herself wondering, with a strange jealousy, if any of her maids had ever led this war-eagle into her palace. The guards made no sign as she led him between them, but he eyed them as a fierce dog might eye a strange pack. She led him through a curtained doorway into an inner chamber, where he stood, naively scanning the tapestries, until he saw a crystal jar of wine on an ebony table. This he took up with a gratified sigh, tilting it toward his lips. Vateesa ran from an inner room, crying breathlessly, "Oh my princess—"

"Princess!"

The wine-jar crashed to the floor. With a motion too quick for sight to follow, the mercenary snatched off Yasmela's veil, glaring. He recoiled with a curse, his sword leaping into his hand with a broad shimmer of blue steel. His eyes blazed like a trapped tiger's. The air was supercharged with tension that was like the pause before the bursting of a storm. Vateesa sank to the floor, speechless with terror, but Yasmela faced the infuriated barbarian without flinching. She realized her very life hung in the balance: maddened with suspicion and unreasoning panic, he was ready to deal death at the slightest provocation. But she experienced a certain breathless exhilaration in the crisis.

"Do not be afraid," she said. "I am Yasmela, but there is no reason to fear me."

"Why did you lead me here?" he snarled, his blazing eyes darting all about the chamber. "What manner of trap is this?"

"There is no trickery," she answered. "I brought you here because you can aid me. I called on the gods—on

Mitra—and he bade me go into the streets and ask aid of the first man I met."

This was something he could understand. The barbarians had their oracles. He lowered his sword, though he did not sheathe it.

"Well, if you're Yasmela, you need aid," he grunted. "Your kingdom's in a devil of a mess. But how can I aid you? If you want a throat cut, of course—"

"Sit down," she requested. "Vateesa, bring him wine."

He complied, taking care, she noticed, to sit with his back against a solid wall, where he could watch the whole chamber. He laid his naked sword across his mail-sheathed knees. She glanced at it in fascination. Its dull blue glimmer seemed to reflect tales of bloodshed and rapine; she doubted her ability to lift it, yet she knew that the mercenary could wield it with one hand as lightly as she could wield a riding-whip. She noted the breadth and power of his hands; they were not the stubby undeveloped paws of a troglodyte. With a guilty start she found herself imagining those strong fingers locked in her dark hair.

He seemed reassured when she deposited herself on a satin divan opposite him. He lifted off his basinet and laid it on the table, and drew back his coif, letting the mail folds fall upon his massive shoulders. She saw more fully now his unlikeness to the Hyborian races. In his dark, scarred face there was a suggestion of moodiness; and without being marked by depravity, or definitely evil, there was more than a suggestion of the sinister about his features, set off by his smoldering blue eyes. A low broad forehead was topped by a square-cut tousled mane as black as a raven's wing.

"Who are you?" she asked abruptly.

"Conan, a captain of the mercenary spearmen," he answered, emptying the wine-cup at a gulp and holding it out for more. "I was born in Cimmeria."

The name meant little to her. She only knew vaguely that it was a wild grim hill-country which lay far to the north, beyond the last outposts of the Hyborian nations, and was peopled by a fierce moody race. She had never before seen one of them.

Resting her chin on her hands, she gazed at him with the deep dark eyes that had enslaved many a heart.

"Conan of Cimmeria," she said, "you said I needed aid. Why?"

"Well," he answered, "any man can see that. Here is the king your brother in an Ophirean prison; here is Koth plotting to enslave you; here is this sorcerer screaming hell-fire and destruction down in Shem—and what's worse, here are your soldiers deserting every day."

She did not at once reply; it was a new experience for a man to speak so forthrightly to her, his words not couched in courtier phrases.

"Why are my soldiers deserting, Conan?" she asked.

"Some are being hired away by Koth," he replied, pulling at the wine-jar with relish. "Many think Khoraja is doomed as an independent state. Many are frightened by tales of this dog Natohk."

"Will the mercenaries stand?" she asked anxiously.

"As long as you pay us well," he answered frankly. "Your politics are nothing to us. You can trust Amalric, our general, but the rest of us are only common men who love loot. If you pay the ransom Ophir asks, men say you'll be unable to pay us. In that case we might go over to the king of Koth, though that cursed miser is no friend of mine. Or we might loot this city. In a civil war the plunder is always plentiful."

"Why would you not go over to Natohk?" she inquired.

"What could he pay us?" he snorted. "With fat-bellied brass idols he looted from the Shemite cities? As long as you're fighting Natohk, you may trust us."

"Would your comrades follow you?" she asked abruptly.

"What do you mean?"

"I mean," she answered deliberately, "that I am going to make you commander of the armies of Khoraja!"

He stopped short, the goblet at his lips, which curved in a broad grin. His eyes blazed with a new light.

"Commander? Crom! But what will your perfumed nobles say?"

"They will obey me!" She clasped her hands to summon a slave, who entered, bowing deeply. "Have Count Thespides come to me at once, and the chancellor Taurus, lord Amalric, and the Agha Shupras.

"I place my trust in Mitra," she said, bending her gaze on Conan, who was now devouring the food placed before him by the trembling Vateesa. "You have seen much war?"

"I was born in the midst of a battle," he answered, tearing a chunk of meat from a huge joint with his strong teeth. "The first sound my ears heard was the clang of swords and the yells of the slaying. I have fought in blood-feuds, tribal wars, and imperial campaigns."

"But can you lead men and arrange battle-lines?"

"Well, I can try," he returned imperturbably. "It's no more than sword-play on a larger scale. You draw his guard, then stab, slash! And either his head is off, or yours."

The slave entered again, announcing the arrival of the men sent for, and Yasmela went into the outer chamber, drawing the velvet curtains behind her. The nobles bent the knee, in evident surprize at her summons at such an hour.

"I have summoned you to tell you of my decision," said Yasmela. "The kingdom is in peril—"

"Right enough, my princess." It was Count Thespides who spoke—a tall man, whose black locks were curled and scented. With one white hand he smoothed his pointed mustache, and with the other he held a velvet chaperon with a scarlet feather fastened by a golden clasp. His pointed shoes were satin, his cote-hardie of gold-broidered velvet. His manner was slightly affected, but the thews under his silks were steely. "It were well to offer Ophir more gold for your royal brother's release."

"I strongly disagree," broke in Taurus the chancellor, an elderly man in an ermine-fringed robe, whose features were lined with the cares of his long service. "We have already offered what will beggar the kingdom to pay. To offer more would further excite Ophir's cupidity. My princess, I say as I have said before: Ophir will not move until we have met this invading horde. If we lose, he will give king Khossus to Koth; if we win, he will doubtless restore his majesty to us on payment of the ransom."

"And in the meantime," broke in Amalric, "the soldiers desert daily, and the mercenaries are restless to know why we dally." He was a Nemedian, a large man with a lion-like yellow mane. "We must move swiftly, if at all—"

"Tomorrow we march southward," she answered. "And there is the man who shall lead you!"

Jerking aside the velvet curtains she dramatically indicated the Cimmerian. It was perhaps not an entirely happy moment for the disclosure. Conan was sprawled in his chair, his feet propped on the ebony table, busily engaged in gnawing a beef-bone which he gripped firmly in both hands.

He glanced casually at the astounded nobles, grinned faintly at Amalric, and went on munching with undisguised relish.

"Mitra protect us!" exploded Amalric. "That's Conan the northron, the most turbulent of all my rogues! I'd have hanged him long ago, were he not the best swordsman that ever donned hauberk—"

"Your highness is pleased to jest!" cried Thespides, his aristocratic features darkening. "This man is a savage—a fellow of no culture or breeding! It is an insult to ask gentlemen to serve under him! I—"

"Count Thespides," said Yasmela, "you have my glove under your baldric. Please give it to me, and then go."

"Go?" he cried, starting. "Go where?"

"To Koth or to Hades!" she answered. "If you will not serve me as I wish, you shall not serve me at all."

"You wrong me, princess," he answered, bowing low, deeply hurt. "I would not forsake you. For your sake I will even put my sword at the disposal of this savage."

"And you, my lord Amalric?"

Amalric swore beneath his breath, then grinned. True soldier of fortune, no shift of fortune, however outrageous, surprized him much.

"I'll serve under him. A short life and a merry one, say I—and with Conan the Throat-slitter in command, life is likely to be both merry and short. Mitra! If the dog ever commanded more than a company of cut-throats before, I'll eat him, harness and all!"

"And you, my Agha?" she turned to Shupras.

He shrugged his shoulders resignedly. He was typical of the race evolved along Koth's southern borders—tall and gaunt, with features leaner and more hawk-like than his purer-blooded desert kin.

"Ishtar gives, princess." The fatalism of his ancestors spoke for him.

"Wait here," she commanded, and while Thespides fumed and gnawed his velvet cap, Taurus muttered wearily under his breath, and Amalric strode back and forth, tugging at his yellow beard and grinning like a hungry lion, Yasmela disappeared again through the curtains and clapped her hands for her slaves.

At her command they brought harness to replace Conan's chain-mail—gorget, sollerets, cuirass, pauldrons, jambes, cuisses and sallet. When Yasmela again drew the curtains, a Conan in burnished steel stood before his audience. Clad in the plate-armor, vizor lifted and dark face shadowed by the black plumes that nodded above his helmet, there was a grim impressiveness about him that even Thespides grudgingly noted. A jest died suddenly on Amalric's lips.

"By Mitra," said he slowly, "I never expected to see you cased in coat-armor, but you do not put it to shame. By my fingerbones, Conan, I have seen kings who wore their harness less regally than you!"

Conan was silent. A vague shadow crossed his mind like a prophecy. In years to come he was to remember Amalric's words, when the dream became the reality.

CHAPTER III

In the early haze of dawn the streets of Khoraja were thronged by crowds of people who watched the hosts riding from the southern gate. The army was on the move at last. There were the knights, gleaming in richly wrought plate-armor, colored plumes waving above their burnished sallets. Their steeds, caparisoned with silk, lacquered leather and gold buckles, caracoled and curvetted as their riders put them through their paces. The early light struck glints from lance-points that rose like a forest above the array, their pennons flowing in the breeze. Each knight wore a lady's token, a glove, scarf or rose, bound to his helmet or fastened to his sword-belt. They were the chivalry of Khoraja, five hundred strong, led by Count Thespides, who, men said, aspired to the hand of Yasmela herself.

They were followed by the light cavalry on rangy steeds. The riders were typical hillmen, lean and hawk-faced; peaked steel caps were on their heads and chain-mail glinted under their flowing kaftans. Their main weapon was the terrible Shemitish bow, which could send a shaft five hundred paces. There were five thousand of these, and Shupras rode at their head, his lean face moody beneath his spired helmet.

Close on their heels marched the Khoraja spearmen, always comparatively few in any Hyborian state, where men

35

thought cavalry the only honorable branch of service. These, like the knights, were of ancient Kothic blood—sons of ruined families, broken men, penniless youths, who could not afford horses and plate-armor, five hundred of them.

The mercenaries brought up the rear, a thousand horsemen, two thousand spearmen. The tall horses of the cavalry seemed hard and savage as their riders; they made no curvets or gambades. There was a grimly business-like aspect to these professional killers, veterans of bloody campaigns. Clad from head to foot in chain-mail, they wore their vizorless head-pieces over linked coifs. Their shields were unadorned, their long lances without guidons. At their saddle-bows hung battle-axes or steel maces, and each man wore at his hip a long broadsword. The spearmen were armed in much the same manner, though they bore pikes instead of cavalry lances.

They were men of many races and many crimes. There were tall Hyperboreans, gaunt, big-boned, of slow speech and violent natures; tawny-haired Gundermen from the hills of the northwest; swaggering Corinthian renegades; swarthy Zingarians, with bristling black mustaches and fiery tempers; Aquilonians from the distant west. But all, except the Zingarians, were Hyborians.

Behind all came a camel in rich housings, led by a knight on a great war-horse, and surrounded by a clump of picked fighters from the royal house-troops. Its rider, under the silken canopy of the seat, was a slim, silk-clad figure, at the sight of which the populace, always mindful of royalty, threw up its leather cap and cheered wildly.

Conan the Cimmerian, restless in his plate armor, stared at the bedecked camel with no great approval, and spoke to Amalric, who rode beside him, resplendent in chain-mail threaded with gold, golden breastplate and helmet with flowing horsehair crest.

"The princess would go with us. She's supple, but too soft for this work. Anyway, she'll have to get out of these robes."

Amalric twisted his yellow mustache to hide a grin. Evidently Conan supposed Yasmela intended to strap on a sword and take part in the actual fighting, as the barbarian women often fought.

"The women of the Hyborians do not fight like your Cimmerian women, Conan," he said. "Yasmela rides with us to watch the battle. Anyway," he shifted in his saddle and lowered his voice, "between you and me, I have an idea that the princess dares not remain behind. She fears something—"

"An uprising? Maybe we'd better hang a few citizens before we start—"

"No. One of her maids talked—babbled about Something that came into the palace by night and frightened

Yasmela half out of her wits. It's some of Natohk's deviltry, I doubt not. Conan, it's more than flesh and blood we fight!"

"Well," grunted the Cimmerian, "it's better to go meet an enemy than to wait for him."

He glanced at the long line of wagons and camp-followers, gathered the reins in his mailed hand, and spoke from habit the phrase of the marching mercenaries, "Hell or plunder, comrades—march!"

Behind the long train the ponderous gates of Khoraja closed. Eager heads lined the battlements. The citizens well knew they were watching life or death go forth. If the host was overthrown, the future of Khoraja would be written in blood. In the hordes swarming up from the savage south, mercy was a quality unknown.

All day the columns marched, through grassy rolling meadowlands, cut by small rivers, the terrain gradually beginning to slope upward. Ahead of them lay a range of low hills, sweeping in an unbroken rampart from east to west. They camped that night on the northern slopes of those hills, and hook-nosed, fiery-eyed men of the hill tribes came in scores to squat about the fires and repeat news that had come up out of the mysterious desert. Through their tales ran the name of Natohk like a crawling serpent. At his bidding the demons of the air brought thunder and wind and fog, the fiends of the underworld shook the earth with awful roaring. He brought fire out of the air and consumed the gates of walled cities, and burnt armored men to bits of charred bone. His warriors covered the desert with their numbers, and he had five thousand Stygian troops in war-chariots under the rebel prince Kutamun.

Conan listened unperturbed. War was his trade. Life was a continual battle, or series of battles, since his birth. Death had been a constant companion. It stalked horrifically at his side; stood at his shoulder beside the gaming-tables; its bony fingers rattled the wine-cups. It loomed above him, a hooded and monstrous shadow, when he lay down to sleep. He minded its presence no more than a king minds the presence of his cupbearer. Some day its bony grasp would close; that was all. It was enough that he lived through the present.

However, others were less careless of fear than he. Striding back from the sentry lines, Conan halted as a slender cloaked figure stayed him with an outstretched hand.

"Princess! You should be in your tent."

"I could not sleep." Her dark eyes were haunted in the shadow. "Conan, I am afraid!"

"Are there men in the host you fear?" His hand locked on his hilt.

"No man," she shuddered. "Conan, is there anything you fear?"

He considered, tugging at his chin. "Aye," he admitted at last, "the curse of the gods."

Again she shuddered. "I am cursed. A fiend from the abysses has set his mark upon me. Night after night he lurks in the shadows, whispering awful secrets to me. He will drag me down to be his queen in hell. I dare not sleep—he will come to me in my pavilion as he came in the palace. Conan, you are strong keep me with you! I am afraid!"

She was no longer a princess, but only a terrified girl. Her pride had fallen from her, leaving her unashamed in her nakedness. In her frantic fear she had come to him who seemed strongest. The ruthless power that had repelled her, drew her now.

For answer he drew off his scarlet cloak and wrapped it about her, roughly, as if tenderness of any kind were impossible to him. His iron hand rested for an instant on her slender shoulder, and she shivered again, but not with fear. Like an electric shock a surge of animal vitality swept over her at his mere touch, as if some of his superabundant strength had been imparted to her.

"Lie here." He indicated a clean-swept space close to a small flickering fire. He saw no incongruity in a princess lying down on the naked ground beside a campfire, wrapped in a warrior's cloak. But she obeyed without question.

He seated himself near her on a boulder, his broadsword across his knees. With the firelight glinting from his blue steel armor, he seemed like an image of steel—dynamic power for the moment quiescent; not resting, but motionless for

40

the instant, awaiting the signal to plunge again into terrific action. The firelight played on his features, making them seem as if carved out of substance shadowy yet hard as steel. They were immobile, but his eyes smoldered with fierce life. He was not merely a wild man; he was part of the wild, one with the untamable elements of life; in his veins ran the blood of the wolf-pack; in his brain lurked the brooding depths of the northern night; his heart throbbed with the fire of blazing forests.

So, half meditating, half dreaming, Yasmela dropped off to sleep, wrapped in a sense of delicious security. Somehow she knew that no flame-eyed shadow would bend over her in the darkness, with this grim figure from the outlands standing guard above her. Yet once again she wakened, to shudder in cosmic fear, though not because of anything she saw.

It was a low mutter of voices that roused her. Opening her eyes, she saw that the fire was burning low. A feeling of dawn was in the air. She could dimly see that Conan still sat on the boulder; she glimpsed the long blue glimmer of his blade. Close beside him crouched another figure, on which the dying fire cast a faint glow. Yasmela drowsily made out a hooked beak of a nose, a glittering bead of an eye, under a white turban. The man was speaking rapidly in a Shemite dialect she found hard to understand.

"Let Bel wither my arm! I speak truth! By Derketo, Conan, I am a prince of liars, but I do not lie to an old comrade. I swear by the days when we were thieves together in the land of Zamora, before you donned hauberk!

"I saw Natohk; with the others I knelt before him when he made incantations to Set. But I did not thrust my nose in the sand as the rest did. I am a thief of Shumir, and my sight is keener than a weasel's. I squinted up and saw his veil blowing in the wind. It blew aside, and I saw—I saw—Bel aid me, Conan, I say I saw! My blood froze in my veins and my hair stood up. What I had seen burned my soul like a red-hot iron. I could not rest until I had made sure.

"I journeyed to the ruins of Kuthchemes. The door of the ivory dome stood open; in the doorway lay a great serpent, transfixed by a sword. Within the dome lay the body of a man, so shrivelled and distorted I could scarce make it out at first—it was Shevatas, the Zamorian, the only thief in the world I acknowledged as my superior. The treasure was untouched; it lay in shimmering heaps about the corpse. That was all."

"There were no bones—" began Conan.

"There was nothing!" broke in the Shemite passionately. "Nothing! Only the one corpse!"

Silence reigned an instant, and Yasmela shrank with a crawling nameless horror.

"Whence came Natohk?" rose the Shemite's vibrant whisper. "Out of the desert on a night when the world was blind and wild with mad clouds driven in frenzied flight across the shuddering stars, and the howling of the wind was mingled with the shrieking of the spirits of the wastes. Vampires were abroad that night, witches rode naked on the wind, and werewolves howled across the wilderness. On a black camel he came, riding like the wind, and an unholy fire played about him; the cloven tracks of the camel glowed in the darkness. When Natohk dismounted before Set's shrine by the oasis of Aphaka, the beast swept into the night and vanished. And I have talked with tribesmen who swore that it suddenly spread gigantic wings and rushed upwards into the clouds, leaving a trail of fire behind it. No man has seen that camel since that night, but a black brutish manlike shape shambles to Natohk's tent and gibbers to him in the blackness before dawn. I will tell you, Conan, Natohk is— look, I will show you an image of what I saw that day by Shushan when the wind blew aside his veil!"

Yasmela saw the glint of gold in the Shemite's hand, as the men bent closely over something. She heard Conan grunt; and suddenly blackness rolled over her. For the first time in her life, princess Yasmela had fainted.

CHAPTER IV

Dawn was still a hint of whiteness in the east when the army was again on the march. Tribesmen had raced into camp, their steeds reeling from the long ride, to report the desert horde encamped at the Well of Altaku. So through the hills the soldiers pushed hastily, leaving the wagon trains to follow. Yasmela rode with them; her eyes were haunted. The nameless horror had been taking even more awful shape, since she had recognized the coin in the Shemite's hand the night before—one of those secretly molded by the degraded Zugite cult, bearing the features of a man dead three thousand years.

The way wound between ragged cliffs and gaunt crags towering over narrow valleys. Here and there villages perched, huddles of stone huts, plastered with mud. The tribesmen swarmed out to join their kin, so that before they had traversed the hills, the host had been swelled by some three thousand wild archers.

Abruptly they came out of the hills and caught their breath at the vast expanse that swept away to the south. On the southern side the hills fell away sheerly, marking a distinct geographical division between the Kothian uplands and the southern desert. The hills were the rim of the uplands, stretching in an almost unbroken wall. Here they were bare and desolate, inhabited only by the Zaheemi clan, whose duty it was to guard the caravan road. Beyond the hills the desert stretched bare, dusty, lifeless. Yet beyond its horizon lay the Well of Altaku, and the horde of Natohk.

The army looked down on the Pass of Shamla, through which flowed the wealth of the north and the south, and through which had marched the armies of Koth, Khoraja, Shem, Turan and Stygia. Here the sheer wall of the rampart was broken. Promontories ran out into the desert, forming barren valleys, all but one of which were closed on the northern extremity by rugged cliffs. This one was the Pass. It was much like a great hand extended from the hills; two fingers, parted, formed a fanshaped valley. The fingers were represented by a broad ridge on either hand, the outer sides sheer, the inner, steep slopes. The vale pitched upward as it narrowed, to come out on a plateau, flanked by gully-torn slopes. A well was there, and a cluster of stone towers, occupied by the Zaheemis.

There Conan halted, swinging off his horse. He had discarded the plate-armor for the more familiar chain-mail. Thespides reined in and demanded, "Why do you halt?"

"We'll await them here," answered Conan.

"T'were more knightly to ride out and meet them," snapped the count.

"They'd smother us with numbers," answered the Cimmerian. "Besides, there's no water out there. We'll camp on the plateau—"

"My knights and I camp in the valley," retorted Thespides angrily. "We are the vanguard, and we, at least, do not fear a ragged desert swarm."

Conan shrugged his shoulders and the angry nobleman rode away. Amalric halted in his bellowing order, to watch the glittering company riding down the slope into the valley.

"The fools! Their canteens will soon be empty, and they'll have to ride back up to the well to water their horses."

"Let them be," replied Conan. "It goes hard for them to take orders from me. Tell the dog-brothers to ease their harness and rest. We've marched hard and fast. Water the horses and let the men munch."

No need to send out scouts. The desert lay bare to the gaze, though just now this view was limited by low-lying clouds which rested in whitish masses on the southern horizon. The monotony was broken only by a jutting tangle of stone ruins, some miles out on the desert, reputedly the remnants of an ancient Stygian temple. Conan dismounted the archers and ranged them along the ridges, with the wild tribesmen. He stationed the mercenaries and the Khoraji spearmen on the plateau about the well. Farther back, in the angle where the hill road debouched on the plateau, was pitched Yasmela's pavilion.

With no enemy in sight, the warriors relaxed. Basinets were doffed, coifs thrown back on mailed shoulders, belts let out. Rude jests flew back and forth as the fighting-men gnawed beef and thrust their muzzles deep into ale-jugs. Along the slopes the hillmen made themselves at ease, nibbling dates and olives. Amalric strode up to where Conan sat bareheaded on a boulder.

"Conan, have you heard what the tribesmen say about Natohk? They say—Mitra, it's too mad even to repeat. What do you think?"

"Seeds rest in the ground for centuries without rotting, sometimes," answered Conan. "But surely Natohk is a man."

"I am not sure," grunted Amalric. "At any rate, you've arranged your lines as well as a seasoned general could have done. It's certain Natohk's devils can't fall on us unawares. Mitra, what a fog!"

"I thought it was clouds at first," answered Conan. "See how it rolls!"

What had seemed clouds was a thick mist moving northward like a great unstable ocean, rapidly hiding the desert from view. Soon it engulfed the Stygian ruins, and still it rolled onward. The army watched in amazement. It was a thing unprecedented—unnatural and inexplicable.

"No use sending out scouts," said Amalric disgustedly. "They couldn't see anything. Its edges are near the outer flanges of the ridges. Soon the whole Pass and these hills will be masked—"

Conan, who had been watching the rolling mist with growing nervousness, bent suddenly and laid his ear to the earth. He sprang up with frantic haste, swearing.

"Horses and chariots, thousands of them! The ground vibrates to their tread! Ho, there!" His voice thundered out across the valley to electrify the lounging men. "Burganets and pikes, you dogs! Stand to your ranks!"

At that, as the warriors scrambled into their lines, hastily donning head-pieces and thrusting arms through shield-straps, the mist rolled away, as something no longer useful. It did not slowly lift and fade like a natural fog; it simply vanished, like a blown-out flame. One moment the whole desert was hidden with the rolling fleecy billows, piled mountainously, stratum above stratum; the next, the sun shone from a cloudless sky on a naked desert—no longer empty, but thronged with the living pageantry of war. A great shout shook the hills.

At first glance the amazed watchers seemed to be looking down upon a glittering sparkling sea of bronze and gold, where steel points twinkled like a myriad stars. With the lifting of the fog the invaders had halted as if frozen, in long serried lines, flaming in the sun.

First was a long line of chariots, drawn by the great fierce horses of Stygia, with plumes on their heads—snorting and rearing as each naked driver leaned back, bracing his powerful legs, his dusky arms knotted with muscles. The fighting-men in the chariots were tall figures, their hawk-like faces set off by bronze helmets crested with a crescent supporting a golden ball. Heavy bows were in their hands. No common archers these, but nobles of the South, bred to war and the hunt, who were accustomed to bringing down lions with their arrows.

Behind these came a motley array of wild men on half-wild horses—the warriors of Kush, the first of the great black kingdoms of the grasslands south of Stygia. They were shining ebony, supple and lithe, riding stark naked and without saddle or bridle.

After these rolled a horde that seemed to encompass all the desert. Thousands on thousands of the war-like Sons of Shem: ranks of horsemen in scale-mail corselets and cylindrical helmets—the asshuri of Nippr, Shumir and Eruk and their sister cities; wild white-robed hordes—the nomad clans.

Now the ranks began to mill and eddy. The chariots drew off to one side while the main host came uncertainly onward.

Down in the valley the knights had mounted, and now Count Thespides galloped up the slope to where Conan stood. He did not deign to dismount but spoke abruptly from the saddle.

"The lifting of the mist has confused them! Now is the time to charge! The Kushites have no bows and they mask the whole advance. A charge of my knights will crush them back into the ranks of the Shemites, disrupting their formation. Follow me! We will win this battle with one stroke!"

Conan shook his head. "Were we fighting a natural foe, I would agree. But this confusion is more feigned than real, as if to draw us into a charge. I fear a trap."

"Then you refuse to move?" cried Thespides, his face dark with passion.

"Be reasonable," expostulated Conan. "We have the advantage of position—"

With a furious oath Thespides wheeled and galloped back down the valley where his knights waited impatiently.

Amalric shook his head. "You should not have let him return, Conan. I—look there!"

Conan sprang up with a curse. Thespides had swept in beside his men. They could hear his impassioned voice faintly, but his gesture toward the approaching horde was significant enough. In another instant five hundred lances dipped and the steel-clad company was thundering down the valley.

A young page came running from Yasmela's pavilion, crying to Conan in a shrill, eager voice. "My Lord, the princess asks why you do not follow and support Count Thespides?"

"Because I am not so great a fool as he," grunted Conan, reseating himself on the boulder and beginning to gnaw a huge beef-bone.

"You grow sober with authority," quoth Amalric. "Such madness as that was always your particular joy."

"Aye, when I had only my own life to consider," answered Conan. "Now—what in hell—"

The horde had halted. From the extreme wing rushed a chariot, the naked charioteer lashing the steeds like a madman; the other occupant was a tall figure whose robe floated spectrally on the wind. He held in his arms a great vessel of gold and from it poured a thin stream that sparkled in the sunlight. Across the whole front of the desert horde the chariot swept, and behind its thundering wheels was left, like the wake behind a ship, a long thin powdery line that glittered in the sands like the phosphorescent track of a serpent.

"That's Natohk!" swore Amalric. "What hellish seed is he sowing?"

The charging knights had not checked their headlong pace. Another fifty paces and they would crash into the uneven Kushite ranks, which stood motionless, spears lifted. Now the foremost knights had reached the thin line that glittered across the sands. They did not heed that crawling menace. But as the steel-shod hoofs of the horses struck it, it was as when steel strikes flint—but with more terrible result. A terrific explosion rocked the desert, which seemed to split apart along the strewn line with an awful burst of white flame.

In that instant the whole foremost line of the knights was seen enveloped in that flame, horses and steel-clad riders withering in the glare like insects in an open blaze. The next instant the rear ranks were piling up on their charred bodies. Unable to check their headlong velocity, rank after rank crashed into the ruins. With appalling suddenness the charge had turned into a shambles where armored figures died amid screaming, mangled horses.

Now the illusion of confusion vanished as the horde settled into orderly lines. The wild Kushites rushed into the shambles, spearing the wounded, bursting the helmets of the knights with stones and iron hammers. It was all over so quickly that the watchers on the slopes stood dazed; and again the horde moved forward, splitting to avoid the charred waste of corpses. From the hills went up a cry: "We fight not men but devils!"

On either ridge the hillmen wavered. One rushed toward the plateau, froth dripping from his beard.

"Flee, flee!" he slobbered. "Who can fight Natohk's magic?"

With a snarl Conan bounded from his boulder and smote him with the beef-bone; he dropped, blood starting from nose and mouth. Conan drew his sword, his eyes slits of blue bale-fire.

"Back to your posts!" he yelled. "Let another take a backward step and I'll shear off his head! Fight, damn you!"

The rout halted as quickly as it had begun. Conan's fierce personality was like a dash of ice-water in their whirling blaze of terror.

"Take your places," he directed quickly. "And stand to it! Neither man nor devil comes up Shamla Pass this day!"

Where the plateau rim broke to the valley slope the mercenaries braced their belts and gripped their spears. Behind them the lancers sat their steeds, and to one side were stationed the Khoraja spearmen as reserves. To Yasmela, standing white and speechless at the door of her tent, the host seemed a pitiful handful in comparison to the thronging desert horde.

Conan stood among the spearmen. He knew the invaders would not try to drive a chariot charge up the Pass in the teeth of the archers, but he grunted with surprize to see the riders dismounting. These wild men had no supply trains. Canteens and pouches hung at their saddle-peaks. Now they drank the last of their water and threw the canteens away.

"This is the death-grip," he muttered as the lines formed on foot. "I'd rather have had a cavalry charge; wounded horses bolt and ruin formations."

The horde had formed into a huge wedge, of which the tip was the Stygians and the body, the mailed asshuri, flanked by the nomads. In close formation, shields lifted, they rolled onward, while behind them a tall figure in a motionless chariot lifted wide-robed arms in grisly invocation.

As the horde entered the wide valley mouth the hillmen loosed their shafts. In spite of the protective formation, men dropped by dozens. The Stygians had discarded their bows; helmeted heads bent to the blast, dark eyes glaring over the rims of their shields, they came on in an inexorable surge, striding over their fallen comrades. But the Shemites gave back the fire, and the clouds of arrows darkened the skies. Conan gazed over the billowing waves of spears and wondered what new horror the sorcerer would invoke. Somehow he felt that Natohk, like all his kind, was more terrible in defense than in attack; to take the offensive against him invited disaster.

But surely it was magic that drove the horde on in the teeth of death. Conan caught his breath at the havoc wrought in the onsweeping ranks. The edges of the wedge seemed to be melting away, and already the valley was strewn with dead men. Yet the survivors came on like madmen unaware of death. By the very numbers of their bows, they began to swamp the archers on the cliffs. Clouds of shafts sped upward, driving the hillmen to cover. Panic struck at their hearts at that unwavering advance, and they plied their bows madly, eyes glaring like trapped wolves.

As the horde neared the narrower neck of the Pass, boulders thundered down, crushing men by the scores, but the charge did not waver. Conan's wolves braced themselves for the inevitable concussion. In their close formation and superior armor, they took little hurt from the arrows. It was the impact of the charge Conan feared, when the huge wedge should crash against his thin ranks. And he realized now there was no breaking of that onslaught. He gripped the shoulder of a Zaheemi who stood near.

"Is there any way by which mounted men can get down into the blind valley beyond that western ridge?"

"Aye, a steep, perilous path, secret and eternally guarded. But—"

Conan was dragging him along to where Amalric sat his great war-horse.

"Amalric!" he snapped. "Follow this man! He'll lead you into yon outer valley. Ride down it, circle the end of the ridge, and strike the horde from the rear. Speak not, but go! I know it's madness, but we're doomed anyway; we'll do all the damage we can before we die! Haste!"

Amalric's mustache bristled in a fierce grin, and a few moments later his lancers were following the guide into a tangle of gorges leading off from the plateau. Conan ran back to the pikemen, sword in hand.

He was not too soon. On either ridge Shupras's hillmen, mad with anticipation of defeat, rained down their shafts desperately. Men died like flies in the valley and along the slopes—and with a roar and an irresistible upward surge the Stygians crashed against the mercenaries.

In a hurricane of thundering steel, the lines twisted and swayed. It was war-bred noble against professional soldier.

Shields crashed against shields, and between them spears drove in and blood spurted.

Conan saw the mighty form of prince Kutamun across the sea of swords, but the press held him hard, breast to breast with dark shapes that gasped and slashed. Behind the Stygians the asshuri were surging and yelling.

On either hand the nomads climbed the cliffs and came to hand-grips with their mountain kin. All along the crests of the ridges the combat raged in blind, gasping ferocity. Tooth and nail, frothing mad with fanaticism and ancient feuds, the tribesmen rent and slew and died. Wild hair flying, the naked Kushites ran howling into the fray.

It seemed to Conan that his sweat-blinded eyes looked down into a rising ocean of steel that seethed and eddied, filling the valley from ridge to ridge. The fight was at a bloody deadlock. The hillmen held the ridges, and the mercenaries, gripping their dipping pikes, bracing their feet in the bloody earth, held the Pass. Superior position and armor for a space balanced the advantage of overwhelming numbers. But it could not endure. Wave after wave of glaring faces and flashing spears surged up the slope, the asshuri filling the gaps in the Stygian ranks.

Conan looked to see Amalric's lancers rounding the western ridge, but they did not come, and the pikemen began to reel back under the shocks. And Conan abandoned all hope of victory and of life. Yelling a command to his gasping captains, he broke away and raced across the plateau to the Khoraja reserves who stood trembling with eagerness. He did not glance toward Yasmela's pavilion. He had forgotten the princess; his one thought was the wild beast instinct to slay before he died.

"This day you become knights!" he laughed fiercely, pointing with his dripping sword toward the hillmen's horses, herded nearby. "Mount and follow me to hell!"

The hill steed reared wildly under the unfamiliar clash of the Kothic armor, and Conan's gusty laugh rose above the din as he led them to where the eastern ridge branched away from the plateau. Five hundred footmen—pauper patricians, younger sons, black sheep—on half-wild Shemite horses, charging an army, down a slope where no cavalry had ever dared charge before!

Past the battle-choked mouth of the Pass they thundered, out onto the corpse-littered ridge. Down the steep slope they rushed, and a score lost their footing and rolled under the hoofs of their comrades. Below them men screamed and threw up their arms—and the thundering charge ripped through them as an avalanche cuts through a forest of saplings. On through the close-packed throngs the Khorajis hurtled, leaving a crushed-down carpet of dead.

And then, as the horde writhed and coiled upon itself, Amalric's lancers, having cut through a cordon of horsemen encountered in the outer valley, swept around the extremity of the western ridge and smote the host in a steel-tipped wedge, splitting it asunder. His attack carried all the dazing demoralization of a surprize on the rear. Thinking themselves flanked by a superior force and frenzied at the fear of being cut off from the desert, swarms of nomads broke and stampeded, working havoc in the ranks of their more steadfast comrades. These staggered and the horsemen rode through them. Up on the ridges the desert fighters wavered, and the hillmen fell on them with renewed fury, driving them down the slopes.

Stunned by surprize, the horde broke before they had time to see it was but a handful which assailed them. And once broken, not even a magician could weld such a horde again. Across the sea of heads and spears Conan's madmen saw Amalric's riders forging steadily through the rout, to the rise and fall of axes and maces, and a mad joy of victory exalted each man's heart and made his arm steel.

Bracing their feet in the wallowing sea of blood whose crimson waves lapped about their ankles, the pikemen in the Pass mouth drove forward, crushing strongly against the milling ranks before them. The Stygians held, but behind them the press of the asshuri melted; and over the bodies of the nobles of the South who died in their tracks to a man, the mercenaries rolled, to split and crumple the wavering mass behind.

Up on the cliffs old Shupras lay with an arrow through his heart; Amalric was down, swearing like a pirate, a spear through his mailed thigh. Of Conan's mounted infantry, scarce a hundred and fifty remained in the saddle. But the horde was shattered. Nomads and mailed spearmen broke away, fleeing to their camp where their horses were, and the hillmen swarmed down the slopes, stabbing the fugitives in the back, cutting the throats of the wounded.

In the swirling red chaos a terrible apparition suddenly appeared before Conan's rearing steed. It was prince Kutamun, naked but for a loin-cloth, his harness hacked away, his crested helmet dented, his limbs splashed with blood. With a terrible shout he hurled his broken hilt full into Conan's face, and leaping, seized the stallion's bridle. The Cimmerian reeled in his saddle, half stunned, and with awful strength the dark-skinned giant forced the screaming steed upward and backward, until it lost its footing and crashed into the muck of bloody sand and writhing bodies.

Conan sprang clear as the horse fell, and with a roar Kutamun was on him. In that mad nightmare of battle, the barbarian never exactly knew how he killed his man.

He only knew that a stone in the Stygian's hand crashed again and again on his basinet, filling his sight with flashing sparks, as Conan drove his dagger again and again into his foe's body, without apparent effect on the prince's terrible vitality. The world was swimming to Conan's sight, when with a convulsive shudder the frame that strained against his stiffened and then went limp.

Reeling up, blood streaming down his face from under his dented helmet, Conan glared dizzily at the profusion of destruction which spread before him. From crest to crest the dead lay strewn, a red carpet that choked the valley. It was like a red sea, with each wave a straggling line of corpses. They choked the neck of the Pass, they littered the slopes. And down in the desert the slaughter continued, where the survivors of the horde had reached their horses and streamed out across the waste, pursued by the weary victors—and Conan stood appalled as he noted how few of these were left to pursue.

Then an awful scream rent the clamor. Up the valley a chariot came flying, making nothing of the heaped corpses. No horses drew it, but a great black creature that was like a camel. In the chariot stood Natohk, his robes flying; and gripping the reins and lashing like mad, crouched a black anthropomorphic being that might have been a monster ape.

With a rush of burning wind the chariot swept up the corpse-littered slope, straight toward the pavilion where Yasmela stood alone, deserted by her guards in the frenzy of pursuit. Conan, standing frozen, heard her frenzied scream as Natohk's long arm swept her up into the chariot. Then the grisly steed wheeled and came racing back down the valley, and no man dared speed arrow or spear lest he strike Yasmela, who writhed in Natohk's arms.

With an inhuman cry Conan caught up his fallen sword and leaped into the path of the hurtling horror. But even as his sword went up, the forefeet of the black beast smote him like a thunderbolt and sent him hurtling a score feet away, dazed and bruised. Yasmela's cry came hauntingly to his stunned ears as the chariot roared by.

A yell that had nothing of the human in its timbre rang from his lips as Conan rebounded from the bloody earth and seized the rein of a riderless horse that raced past him, throwing himself into the saddle without bringing the charger to a halt. With mad abandon he raced after the rapidly receding chariot. He struck the levels flying, and passed like a whirlwind through the Shemite camp. Into the desert he fled, passing clumps of his own riders, and hard-spurring desert horsemen.

On flew the chariot, and on raced Conan, though his horse began to reel beneath him. Now the open desert lay all about them, bathed in the lurid desolate splendor of sunset. Before him rose up the ancient ruins, and with a shriek that froze the blood in Conan's veins, the unhuman charioteer cast Natohk and the girl from him. They rolled on the sand, and to Conan's dazed gaze, the chariot and its steed altered awfully. Great wings spread from a black horror that in no way resembled a camel, and it rushed upward into the sky, bearing in its wake a shape of blinding flame, in which a black man-like shape gibbered in ghastly triumph. So quickly it passed, that it was like the rush of a nightmare through a horror-haunted dream.

Natohk sprang up, cast a swift look at his grim pursuer, who had not halted but came riding hard, with sword swinging low and spattering red drops; and the sorcerer caught up the fainting girl and ran with her into the ruins.

Conan leaped from his horse and plunged after them. He came into a room that glowed with unholy radiance, though outside the dusk was falling swiftly. On a black jade altar lay Yasmela, her naked body gleaming like ivory in the weird light. Her garments lay strewn on the floor, as if ripped from her in brutal haste. Natohk faced the Cimmerian— inhumanly tall and lean, clad in shimmering green silk. He tossed back his veil, and Conan looked into the features he had seen depicted on the Zugite coin.

"Aye, blench, dog!" The voice was like the hiss of a giant serpent. "I am Thugra Khotan! Long I lay in my tomb, awaiting the day of awakening and release. The arts which saved me from the barbarians long ago likewise imprisoned me, but I knew one would come in time—and he came, to fulfill his destiny, and to die as no man has died in three thousand years!

"Fool, do you think you have conquered because my people are scattered? Because I have been betrayed and deserted by the demon I enslaved? I am Thugra Khotan, who shall rule the world despite your paltry gods! The desert is filled with my people; the demons of the earth shall do my bidding, as the reptiles of the earth obey me. Lust for a woman weakened my sorcery. Now the woman is mine, and feasting on her soul, I shall be unconquerable! Back, fool! You have not conquered Thugra Khotan!"

He cast his staff and it fell at the feet of Conan, who recoiled with an involuntary cry. For as it fell it altered horribly; its outline melted and writhed, and a hooded cobra reared up hissing before the horrified Cimmerian. With a furious oath Conan struck, and his sword sheared the horrid shape in half. And there at his feet lay only the two pieces of a severed ebon staff. Thugra Khotan laughed awfully, and wheeling, caught up something that crawled loathsomely in the dust of the floor.

In his extended hand something alive writhed and slavered. No tricks of shadows this time. In his naked hand Thugra Khotan gripped a black scorpion, more than a foot in length, the deadliest creature of the desert, the stroke of whose spiked tail was instant death. Thugra Khotan's skull-like countenance split in a mummy-like grin. Conan hesitated; then without warning he threw his sword.

Caught off guard, Thugra Khotan had no time to avoid the cast. The point struck beneath his heart and stood out a foot behind his shoulders. He went down, crushing the poisonous monster in his grasp as he fell.

Conan strode to the altar, lifting Yasmela in his blood-stained arms. She threw her white arms convulsively about his mailed neck, sobbing hysterically, and would not let him go.

"Crom's devils, girl!" he grunted. "Loose me! Fifty thousand men have perished today, and there is work for me to do—"

"No!" she gasped, clinging with convulsive strength, as barbaric for the instant as he in her fear and passion. "I will not let you go! I am yours, by fire and steel and blood! You are mine! Back there, I belong to others—here I am mine—and yours! You shall not go!"

He hesitated, his own brain reeling with the fierce upsurging of his violent passions. The lurid unearthly glow still hovered in the shadowy chamber, lighting ghostlily the dead face of Thugra Khotan, which seemed to grin mirthlessly and cavernously at them. Out on the desert, in the hills among the oceans of dead, men were dying, were howling with wounds and thirst and madness, and kingdoms were staggering. Then all was swept away by the crimson tide that rode madly in Conan's soul, as he crushed fiercely in his iron arms the slim white body that shimmered like a witch-fire of madness before him.

www.ingramcontent.com/pod-product-compliance
Lightning Source LLC
Chambersburg PA
CBHW020919180626
46816CB00007BA/2471